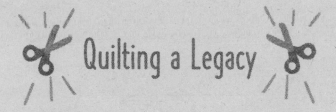

Quilting a Legacy

D0064622

Don't miss the other Invincible Girls Club adventures!

Home Sweet Forever Home
Art with Heart
Back to Nature

THE INVINCIBLE GIRLS CLUB

BOOK 4

by Steph B. Jones and Rachele Alpine

illustrated by Addy Rivera Sonda

Aladdin

New York   London   Toronto   Sydney   New Delhi

ALADDIN

An imprint of Simon & Schuster Children's Publishing Division

1230 Avenue of the Americas, New York, New York 10020

First Aladdin paperback edition July 2022

Text copyright © 2022 by Stephanie Jones and Rachele Alpine

Illustrations copyright © 2022 by Addy Rivera Sonda

Also available in an Aladdin hardcover edition.

All rights reserved, including the right of reproduction in whole or in part in any form.

ALADDIN and related logo are registered trademarks of Simon & Schuster, Inc.

For information about special discounts for bulk purchases, please contact Simon & Schuster Special Sales at 1-866-506-1949 or business@simonandschuster.com.

The Simon & Schuster Speakers Bureau can bring authors to your live event. For more information or to book an event contact the Simon & Schuster Speakers Bureau at 1-866-248-3049 or visit our website at www.simonspeakers.com.

Book designed by Heather Palisi and Ginny Kemmerer

The illustrations for this book were rendered digitally.

The text of this book was set in Celeste.

Manufactured in the United States of America 0622 OFF

2 4 6 8 10 9 7 5 3 1

Library of Congress Cataloging-in-Publication Data

Names: Jones, Steph B., author. | Alpine, Rachele, 1979- author. | Sonda, Addy Rivera, illustrator.

Title: Quilting a legacy / by Steph B. Jones and Rachele Alpine ; illustrated by Addy Rivera Sonda.

Description: First Aladdin paperback edition. | New York : Aladdin, 2022. | Series: The invincible girls club ; book 4 | Audience: Ages 7 to 10. | Summary: Myka signs her gammy and three best friends up for quilting classes, but for someone who is used to being the best at each activity she tries, Myka finds quilting surprisingly challenging.

Identifiers: LCCN 2022010475 (print) | LCCN 2022010476 (ebook) | ISBN 9781665921398 (hc) | ISBN 9781665921381 (pbk) | ISBN 9781665921404 (ebook)

Subjects: CYAC: Quilting—Fiction. | Grandmothers—Fiction. | Best friends—Fiction. | Friendship—Fiction. | LCGFT: Fiction.

Classification: LCC PZ7.1.J743 Qu 2022 (print) | LCC PZ7.1.J743 (ebook) | DDC [Fic]—dc23

LC record available at https://lccn.loc.gov/2022010475

LC ebook record available at https://lccn.loc.gov/2022010476

For Nanny . . .
whose good food and stories still feed my soul.
Guess I'll never know how a pinch of this or that turns
into delicious, soul-food Sunday dinners.
—S. B. J.

*You, be it. Be about it. Be about that action,
and go do it!*
—Beyoncé

Contents

ON PINS AND NEEDLES

"She's here!" I yelled, and pushed past my brother Remy, knocking him to the ground. "Gammy is here!"

Before Remy could complain of a concussion, I swung open the front door and raced toward her. I glanced back, catching a glimpse of Remy rubbing his head. When I turned around, I almost crashed into Dad, who was carrying most of Gammy's bags.

"Easy now, track star." Dad lifted the duffel bags over my head.

I didn't stop sprinting until I reached the edge of the walkway.

"Finally!" I cheered.

I smiled wide, threw my arms around Gammy's waist, and pulled her in for a big hug. One of those I-haven't-seen-you-in-person-for-a-year hugs. Gammy smelled so good. Not like she'd been sitting on the plane for three hours but like she'd been baking peanut butter chocolate chip cookies instead.

"Took you long enough!" I joked.

"Guess I should stay away more often." Gammy gave me a squeeze, a kiss on the cheek, and then a pat on the bottom.

"Gammy, I have so much to tell you. So many things to show you." My words flew out a mile a minute.

I sure hoped Gammy had slept on the plane. We had things to do and people to meet—in person and not over a video chat. In real life no one gets frozen.

Mom helped Gammy up the last two steps into the house.

"First things first," I said. "We have to go to the cupcake shop and meet up with the other Invincible Girls—"

"Sweetie, calm yourself." Mom shot me the *Myka, bring it down* look. The one she gives me when I need to turn my energy down a notch— her words, not mine.

But I couldn't help it—Gammy was here. That meant exciting outings, lots of laughs, amazing stories, and good food. Gammy was staying with us for five weeks. If I was lucky, I might convince her to stay longer.

"Gammy, did you bring anything cool? What are you cooking?" Questions fired out of me like I was in the three-point hoop contest and there were ten seconds left on the clock.

"Let your grandmother put down her purse and get settled," Mom said.

Dad handed Gammy's duffel bag to one of my other brothers, Jordan.

"Yeah, Myka, it's not a competition for Gammy's attention!" Jordan added.

I bit my tongue and wrapped my curls up in a bun. The last thing I wanted to do was get into trouble while Gammy was here.

"Leave your sister alone. I missed her too." Gammy kissed my cheek and then playfully wagged her finger at my brother. "There was a time when you were just as hyper and excited about my visits as Myka."

It was so good to have Gammy here. Even though my friends in the Invincible Girls Club thought I was outspoken, always confident, and not a pushover, that wasn't always the case. Sometimes it felt like no one understood me, especially at home.

Mom was a super-girly girl, and my brothers . . .

well, it's eat or be eaten with those guys. But Gammy grew up an only girl who loved sports as much as she liked dresses. She wanted to be a princess and a professional baseball player. And I wanted to be a video game designer and play soccer in the Olympics.

I settled into a seat across from Gammy at the kitchen table. Remy sat down and stuck out his tongue at me.

"Mom said you're staying five weeks, Gammy. Is that true?" he asked.

Remy held a frozen bag of broccoli up to his head.

"Trying to get rid of me already?"

Remy shook his head.

"Never, Gammy. Wish you'd move in," my older brother Alex said.

"You guys are growing up just fine. Don't need old Gammy getting in the way."

Remy got up and put his head on her shoulder. I rolled my eyes at him.

Getting Gammy all to myself wasn't going to be easy. Why must they turn everything into a competition?

"What do you want us to do with this box?" Dad placed a large green-and-yellow-flowered box on the table in front of Gammy.

My eyes lit up and questions flooded my brain. She tapped the mahogany-colored wooden box with gold-plated edges with her left hand. "Just leave it here for now."

"What's in the box?" Jordan asked.

Gammy gave him a sneaky look. "You'll find out."

"Tell us now?" I asked.

"Not now, but soon."

Gammy never came with gifts, only stories. And I talked to her all the time, about everything. Surely we didn't have any secrets. I needed to find out what was in the box.

Gammy stared at me as she took the box off the table.

"I can see your mind working. Don't think too much about the box, Myka."

With the box in both hands, Gammy left the kitchen. Not knowing was like torture.

I snuck behind Gammy and followed her upstairs, then peeked around the corner. She went into my bedroom with all her luggage, because Gammy and I were roommates for her visit. My eyes followed the box. The instrumental of "Take Me Out to the Ball Game" played for a few seconds; then I heard Gammy's voice. "I made it here safely. . . . Yes, I have the box."

I inched closer toward the door, which was closed almost all the way. Just like I thought, this box was important. I almost stopped breathing when Gammy came and stood by the door. I didn't want her to think I was being sneaky. My body tensed.

"Yes, I'm going to tell Myka everything."

I clasped my hands over my mouth. *What does she have to tell me?* Moments later my bedroom door opened and Gammy walked out humming, wearing a shower cap on her head and holding a towel and a robe.

Perfect.

I had ten minutes to snoop.

I waited a few moments before walking into the room. The box sat right in the middle of the bed and called to me like a Christmas present.

I was just going to take a quick peek into the box.

I let out my breath.

One peek wouldn't hurt.

Gammy had been keeping secrets. And other than birthday gifts, secrets weren't usually good. *Please don't let it be that Mom is getting stationed somewhere else and we're moving again,* I thought. If that were the case, then Gammy's extended visit, along with whatever was in the box, was supposed to soften the blow. But I didn't think even that would help me hide my disappointment if I had to up and leave. I loved our town and the other Invincible Girls. I turned the box toward me and was surprised to discover that it had a lock, but before I could examine the box more closely, someone came in. It was Gammy, now wearing her plush baseball robe but she couldn't fool me. Her shower cap was dry as a bone. There was no way she showered.

A TRUTH SEW AMAZING

2

The guilt was making jumbo-size pretzel knots in my stomach. Mom had told me it wasn't right to look through people's belongings without their permission. And I hadn't listened. Time to confess. I sat in the middle of the bed, gripping the now-larger-than-life box in my sweaty hands.

"You just couldn't wait, huh?" Gammy smirked, then sat next to me on the bed.

"No." I pushed the box toward Gammy with my head hung low, afraid to look her in the eye.

Gammy sucked in a deep breath. "I should've known any granddaughter of mine wouldn't have wanted to wait for her *secret* surprise."

She unhooked a chain from around her neck. She'd been wearing the key the whole time. That was genius. Man, I hoped I'd be as smart as Gammy when I grew up.

"I'm sorry."

"Don't be sorry for being inquisitive. Be sorry for being nosy." Gammy laughed.

And I did too. Our laughter warmed me up like hot chocolate does on a cold winter's day.

Gammy wasn't mad after all. I was safe.

Not only that, but she was unlocking the box and lifting up the lid!

I couldn't believe it; I was going to see what was inside!

"Okay, pay attention. What I'm about to show you is some of my most cherished stuff," she said.

One by one Gammy shared each item with

me. The box was filled with memories and trinkets from her childhood. She even had some square thing she called a floppy disk. Not sure what it did. And Gammy couldn't remember why she'd kept it, but it looked cool. She placed each treasured item on the bed in a row until there were only two things still left in the box.

"What's this?" I asked.

Gammy set a sealed plastic bag on her lap. "This is what I'm most excited to share with you."

"Is this what you were talking about on the phone?"

Gammy laughed. "Little birdies sure do have big ears."

"Birdies? Where?" I asked.

Gammy pinched my cheek. "Right here, you're the birdie. Now, let me tell you a story."

Gammy slipped a quilt out of the plastic bag and spread it out gently over the bed.

It looked old. And according to Gammy's story, it was. Like, way back in the days of Harriet

Tubman and Frederick Douglass, the abolition-
ists, old.

The white part of the quilt had yellowed, but
the other parts with reds, blues, oranges, and
greens were still filled with color. Then Gammy
told me all about how the women in her family
had learned to make quilts. They passed the tradition down to each daughter born in our family.
Gammy said the quilt she held in her arms was

made for the first baby in our family born free in America.

"Born free? What does that mean?" I asked.

"It means my great-great-grandmother was the first in our bloodline who wasn't born enslaved."

"Wow, and you still have it?" I reached out and traced the patterns and shapes with the tip of my finger, careful not to touch it roughly.

"The women in my family saved and repaired the original baby blanket. Then each mother added squares, making the quilt larger. With each new border came more stories passed down along with the quilt. You could say it helps keep our family's legacy alive."

I ran my hands across the different rectangular and triangular patterns.

"This quilt has been all up and down the East Coast from Florida to New York. Now it is here with you." Gammy pinched my nose.

"Which squares did you make for Mommy?"

"None," she said in a quiet voice.

Gammy grabbed a large mesh packing cube from her suitcase. At first glance the stuff inside the cube looked like rags, but it was squares made from baby clothes, old T-shirts, and worn clothing.

"Why not?" I asked.

"Because my mom never got the chance to teach me. But I always figured I'd learn, so I saved these pieces." Gammy's voice was low, almost a whisper.

She kissed my cheek. "Our original family quilt is too old and fragile to try to add more squares. For years, I've been saving scraps of sentimental clothes from your mom's childhood. No specific plan in mind. But I always wanted to make something special."

I glanced back and forth between the completed family quilt and Gammy's. The one Gammy was making reminded me of something that would be on her couch in her living room. The bright colors and patterns were bold just like her. The family quilt was softer, the colors less vibrant but deep and rich. It looked like something that belonged in a Smithsonian museum. Then, just like that, a brilliant idea popped into my head.

"Gammy, let's learn how to make quilts! That way we can continue our family legacy. If we can't add to the original family quilt because it's too delicate, let's make another one!"

"Make our own quilt—just like that, huh?" Gammy said, and laughed, but I was serious.

"You're here for over a month; we could totally do this! Does Mom need to learn too? It could be our special girls' thing!"

"That's not a bad idea. Count me in."

"Awesome," I said. "Okay. Now all I have to do is find a quilting coach. I mean teacher."

If Gammy and I were going to learn to make quilts, then we'd have to spend lots of time together, which was quite all right with me.

I noticed there was one item left in the box.

It looked like an old piece of notepad paper. The name "Mary L. King" written in bold cursive under the heading *NACA* caught my eye. I searched my brain, running through memories like a search engine. But I had no clue what those letters stood for.

I pulled the paper out of the box.

"Why did you save this paper with scribbles all over it? And what is NACA?"

Gammy laughed. "It's not scribbles. It's numbers—equations, to be exact. My aunt Mary was a mathematician."

"Like a math teacher?"

"No, like a scientist. Those letters, *N-A-C-A*, are now known as 'NASA.'"

My eyes widened. "Like outer space NASA?"

"Like out of this world."

"You have to tell me all about her." I set the paper inside the box and scooted back on the bed. If I had my choice, I'd sit there and listen to Gammy's stories all day long. Especially since my brothers weren't there to interrupt her with fart noises and silly gossip questions about all the professional athletes she'd met as a sports trainer for the Yankees and nothing about how they stayed at the top of their game.

Gammy stood up. "My sweet little Myka, that is a story for later."

3 SHARING IS HARDER THAN IT SEAMS

"Myka, you've had your hand raised for a while," Miss Taylor said. "Is there something you'd like to share with the class before lunch?"

"Yes." I look at the other Invincible Girls—Lauren, Ruby, and Emelyn—all seated near me. "My grandmother is visiting us, and yesterday she showed me an item that has been passed down in my family since the days of Frederick Douglass."

Miss Taylor's eyes lit up with interest.

Every set of eyeballs in the class was now

glued on me. I quivered. Without a ball in my hand, or a friend to defend, I didn't like to be the center of attention. Maybe I should have just let her dismiss us for lunch and shown Miss Taylor in private. No, I couldn't do that. I knew that if Gammy were there, she'd say, *Ain't nothing to it but to do it.*

Plus, I really enjoyed Miss Taylor's Little-Known Agents of Change lessons. She'd been teaching mini lessons on various Americans who have helped make our country what it is today but oftentimes got overlooked. Miss Taylor would end each of these lessons by asking one of us to share a story of an agent of change in our family. Before, I would hide behind my notebook or scribble while silently hoping not to get called on, but that stopped today. Finally I could share something about my family.

"Wow, that is very cool," Miss Taylor said.

"Oh, and I also learned that my great-great-aunt used to work at NASA back when it was called 'NACA.'"

"Myka is making this up," Nelson shouted.

"Nelson, remember, if you don't have anything nice to say, it's best to keep your thoughts to yourself," Miss Taylor said.

If ever there was a person I'd have liked to strike out, it was Nelson. Because I was always beating him on any field or court we played on, he was always trying to battle me in the classroom.

"Myka is an Invincible Girl. And we don't lie," Emelyn shot back at him.

"That's right," Lauren added.

It was good to know that the girls in the IG club always have each other's backs. I sat up extra straight.

"Look, I have proof." I pulled out my tablet with photos of Gammy and me holding the quilt and the piece of paper with my great-great-aunt Mary's name on it.

"That is gorgeous," Miss Taylor said. "My cousin quilts, and her talent amazes me. She's always trying to get me to learn."

"My family has been quilting for centuries," I told her proudly.

"It is truly remarkable that your family has been able to save this. Sounds like you will have a lot to add and share when we get to Women's History Month lessons," Miss Taylor said.

Ruby's hand shot up into the air. "Miss Taylor, would that make Myka's great-great-aunt a hidden figure? You know, like Katherine Johnson

 23

and the other Black female scientists you taught us about? The ones who were hidden in the background but their math problem-solving helped put a spaceship into outer space?"

Miss Taylor smiled. "Excellent connection, Ruby. Absolutely. Myka's family member was a hidden figure. But now that we have all learned about her, she's no longer hidden." Miss Taylor winked at me.

It felt good to be more than the girl whose family moved a lot because her mom was in the military. Or the girl with all the brothers who also loved sports. It felt like I had roots. I was a part of history.

"Thanks again for sharing, Myka. What a special way to close our Agents of Change lessons." Miss Taylor clapped her hands. "And now it's time for lunch."

My classmates didn't hesitate to get in line and make a mad dash to the cafeteria. Emelyn, Lauren, and Ruby waited for me.

"That was so cool, Myka," Ruby said. "Aren't grandmas the best? My grandma is like my best adult friend. I'm always downstairs hanging out in her apartment knitting and watching TV with her!"

"Agreed," I replied. "Gammy is mine too. I can't wait for the three of you to meet her. Let's ask our moms if you guys can come over for Sunday dinner so you can have some soul food."

"What's soul food?" Lauren asked.

"It's good food for the soul: collard greens, corn bread, mac and cheese, and smothered turkey wings or fried chicken," I gushed.

"Let's walk and talk. You're making me hungry," Ruby said.

"Same here," Emelyn chimed in. "That sounds delish."

Gammy's visit had come right on time. I'd been waiting to share my family's soul food with the other Invincible Girls.

The four of us talked and laughed all the way through lunch and into recess.

Other than the science lab, the playground was the best place in the whole school. Any sport you wanted to play could happen there. And out there was where I felt like I belonged. My oldest brother, Jordan, had said that sports was one of the few things that brings everyone, regardless of their differences, together.

"Invincible Girls, I need your help," I told them as the four of us climbed on the tire swing together.

"What do you need?" Emelyn asked. "You know you've always got our help."

"Gammy needs to learn how to quilt."

"I thought she already knew how. The picture of the quilt you shared was amazing," Emelyn said.

"All the women in my family before knew how. But she never got to learn. Her mom passed away before she could teach Gammy. And after that, it wasn't so easy for Gammy to return to the quilt because of the memories."

Lauren gave me a gentle smile. "That would have been hard."

"Yep, still is," I replied. "That's where I come in. I want to help her carry on our family legacy. We're making a new family quilt."

"That's such a great idea!" Ruby said.

I nodded, but not with the same enthusiasm as Ruby. "It would be, but there's only one problem."

"What's that?" asked Lauren.

"I have no idea how to quilt. Do any of you know someone who does?" I asked, and my stomach sank as I watched each of them one by one shake their heads.

"Have no fear!" Ruby exclaimed. "The Invincible Girls Club is here, and we've got you covered! Get it? Covered? Like a quilt?"

"Oh yeah, we've sew got this!" Lauren joked. "*S-E-W*, I mean!"

We all groaned, but in that moment, I was reminded of how much my friends' love really did blanket me. And with that, I giggled once again at Lauren's pun and spun us around and around on the tire swing.

With the other Invincible Girls' help, there was no doubt Gammy and I would learn how to sew and make a new family quilt.

MY FAMILY LEAVES ME IN STITCHES

4

"**H**ow was school today, Sweet Pea?" Mom asked as she pinched my cheek. Then she pulled out of the school's pickup line. Mom hardly ever picked me up, because she usually worked late. My big brother Jordan usually scooped me up with a car full of his sweaty teammates on their way to get snacks at the Express Mart by our house. So I figured I wouldn't complain about her treating me like a baby in front of the entire school.

"It was fun. I told the class some cool facts about our family before we went to lunch."

"That's great. I heard you telling Gammy that you'd been hiding during those lessons in class," Mom said. Her eyes were fixed on the road, but I knew she could still see me with her side-eye.

"That's not exactly true. When we learned about women in the military who are breaking glass ceilings, I talked about you being one of, like, five Black women at your base. Oh, and the only female psychiatrist in the state."

She laughed so hard, her eyes were almost closed shut. "Now, Myka, you added a lot of sauce to that story. I am not the only one."

"It could be true," I said. "You know I don't really like sharing in class."

It wasn't easy to talk about myself and share personal stories in class, especially because we moved a lot. Now that I had a really great sports team and the other Invincible Girls, I was hoping my moving days were in the past.

"I never would've guessed you didn't like to share. At home your mouth is always running a mile a minute," she joked.

"Very funny," I told her. "That's because I save all my conversations for you."

Mom nodded. "I understand. And believe it or not, I was never much of a talker."

"You sure do a lot of talking now," I joked.

"Excuse me! I can't believe it, my own baby, calling your mom a blabbermouth."

"No way. I just can't picture you, a master sergeant in the air force, being quiet in class."

"When you say it like that, it is pretty funny." We laughed as she cranked up the music. The two of us sang old R&B songs from the nineties all the way home.

When we walked through the door, we were instantly hit with the smell of something amazing.

If you asked me, I'd say Dad was the best

chef in the state. Most of his recipes were his own creation, like Caribbean-style seafood street tacos made on the grill, and tuna broccoli surprise bake. He didn't think I knew this, but his top secret ingredient was Cheez Whiz. His meals were always an event, but now that he was in the kitchen with Gammy having a cook-off, I wasn't so sure Dad would get the high score on this one.

"Gammy, I'm ready to taste your lamb stew. Dad's stew was too spicy," Remy said as he licked his lips like a cartoon character drooling over a meal. All he needed was a bib around his neck and an oversize fork and knife in his hand.

"I'll remember that my lamb stew was too spicy the next time you want seconds and thirds." Dad dried his hands on the Greatest Father in the Galaxy apron we'd made for Father's Day and scooped Remy's head into his arm and playfully shook him.

"Hey, watch my hair. It's just starting to curl," Remy complained.

"You need a haircut," Dad teased.

Gammy pulled Remy in for a hug. "Leave my Remy alone. My grandbaby is looking good, and he knows it."

"If he wants to look good, he can start by smelling good and taking a shower," Jordan joked as he entered the kitchen, slam-dunking a napkin into the garbage. Remy hated to shower; he'd rather run through the sprinklers on the lawn.

I tried to hide my laughter.

"I know you're not talking, Jordan. You didn't start taking showers until Jessica Charles spoke to you during algebra class," Alex shot back at him.

Remy perked up because the brothers' playing field had just leveled out. Alex put his hands on Remy's shoulders.

"Where is your proof?" Jordan asked. He rolled up his sleeves.

I snuck a spoonful of Gammy's lamb stew as I prepared for the next round of the Bader brothers' hike-fest. Mom said that neither Alex nor Jordan had been too fond of showers at Remy's age. I would never understand boys.

"All right, fellas. Let's have some manners," Dad said. "I don't want Gammy to think that your mom and I are raising young men with no dinner table manners."

"Technically we aren't at the dinner table because we haven't sat down yet," Alex replied. "We're still in the kitchen."

Mom folded her arms across her chest. "Did I just hear one of my cadets say they wanted to drop and give me fifty?"

We knew Mom meant business when she started talking to us like we were soldiers.

"No, ma'am," Alex said as Jordan, Remy, and I laughed behind our hands.

"Pipe down there, Sergeant Bader," Gammy said. "I've got the highest rank here now. Besides, there is nothing I haven't seen from young men after my years with baseball players. My grandsons are little angels."

Either Gammy had no idea or she'd got her blinders up. My brothers were far from angels.

"Mom and Dad, I need a favor," I told them as I scooped out another spoonful of Gammy's lamb stew. I was sure Dad's was delicious, but I was not going to pass up an opportunity to eat Gammy's cooking.

"What is it, Sweet Pea? And does it involve money?" Dad asked, and Mom chuckled.

"No, not this time. I'd like to invite the other Invincible Girls and their parents to Sunday dinner."

Mom's eyes immediately looked toward the dining room table, which had everything but space for the dinnerware on it.

"I'll make sure the dining room table looks

company-ready by then, I promise. And I will even help cook for the extra guests."

"Why this weekend? What's the occasion?" Dad asked.

"Well, Gammy's here and I want them to meet her," I told him.

"That's an awful lot of people around our table," Mom said.

"Maybe my brothers can spend the night somewhere else?" I asked.

"Myka!" Dad said, choking back a laugh.

"Just teasing. But it would give us a lot of extra food," I said.

Remy stuck his tongue out while Jordan and Alex smiled and shook their heads.

"We have plenty of room for *everyone*. I'll call all their moms. I'd love to have the other Invincible Girls over for one of our soul-food Sunday meals. And here's hoping your gammy will do us the honor of cooking," Mom said.

Gammy placed her hands on her hips. "I

wouldn't have it any other way. Invite the girls over. We'll share stories and good food. And speaking of food, let's stop sampling and dish this stew and eat like a family!"

Perfect. There was nothing better than when a good idea came together. Now we just needed to figure out how to get Gammy quilting. And fast! She was only here for five weeks. It was time for me to put my head together with the other Invincible Girls and come up with a plan.

5 PIN PALS

There was only one thing I could focus on that day in school: talking to the other Invincible Girls about quilting classes. But we were busy nonstop. There was no time for talking in class. It was just back-to-back work, like a marathon. Third grade was becoming intense. I'd never been happier for recess.

"What's up, Myka?" Lauren asked. "It looked like you were trying to catch our attention all morning."

38

"I was," I confirmed, sitting down on the swing.

"Is it about dinner on Sunday? I heard my mom on the phone with your mom last night," Lauren said.

"No. But I'm so excited about having you all over. I'm still trying to find a place to learn to quilt. But I'm not sure where to look."

"Did you do an online search? That's a good place to start," Ruby offered. "That's where I like to go for any articles I write for our school paper."

None of us had phones or devices linked to Wi-Fi in school.

"I did at home," I told her. "But the videos seemed too confusing. Gammy isn't great with technology, so I think we need to take a class in person."

"That makes sense. Could you look for a class?" Emelyn asked.

"I did, but there were so many, I didn't know which one was good," I told her.

"We need to speak with someone who has personal experience. You know, like someone who has taken a class," Lauren suggested.

"What about Miss Taylor?" Ruby asked. "Remember that she mentioned in class the other day that her cousin quilts?"

"Yes! That's perfect," I said.

"Let's ask her. She may know, and if she doesn't, she can tell us where to look," Ruby added, and I could tell she was excited about the connection she had made.

The four of us took off to the other side of the playground, where Miss Taylor sat eating her fruit.

"Oh, hey, girls. What's up?" she asked when we circled around her table.

"Hey, Miss Taylor. We need your help," I said. Then we filled her in on my plan to learn to quilt with Gammy.

"We remembered you said your cousin quilts," Ruby added.

"Did you four read my mind?" She slipped a piece of paper out of her dress pocket. "After Myka shared her story about quilting with the class, I reached out to my cousin. I had no idea that quilting was such a part of our American history." Miss Taylor handed me the paper.

I read the flyer.

Free Quilting for Beginners

Learn quilting basics in weeks!

Bring your own supplies.

Lessons: Mondays & Wednesdays

Time: 6 p.m. to 8 p.m.

Location: Erie Community Center

"Where's the community center?" I asked.

"It's right in town, not too far from the animal shelter. I've been there before with my grand-mother for bingo night," Ruby said.

I passed the flyer to Ruby, who passed it along to the other girls to read.

"My cousin is teaching the class. She said she usually has just grown-ups in the class, but she'd love to have the four of you," Miss Taylor told us.

"The four of us?" Ruby asked.

"No, no, it would just be me and Gammy," I clarified.

"Actually," Emelyn piped up, "I'd like to take the class too. That's one form of art I haven't tried yet, and my mom has been really busy at work lately. Maybe I can talk her into taking a break and spending some bonding time with me."

"That would be so fun if you and your mom

came!" I told Emelyn, excited at the idea of one of my friends being interested.

"Whoa! Wait a minute," Ruby interrupted. "I don't want to be left out and miss all the fun!"

"The more the merrier!" I said, giddy at the idea of this suddenly becoming not only something the other Invincible Girls helped me with but something that they actually *did* with me.

"I'm not sure if I'll be able to. I usually go with Mom and Scott to take Carter to cross-country on Wednesday nights. It's one of the things we do as a family," Lauren said, her face full of disappointment.

"No problem, that's an easy fix," Emelyn replied. "Whatever you miss, we can help you with the next day at school."

"Oooooh! Allow me to interject." Ruby raised her finger. "Isn't that word cool? Just sounds so fancy. Why say 'cut in' when you can 'interject'?"

We laughed.

"What if we quilted during our lunch period?

That would be the perfect activity to do if we can't go outside during recess. I just heard we've got some rainy days headed our way," Ruby suggested.

"You girls are so resourceful!" Miss Taylor said, and we all instantly turned toward Ruby, our walking dictionary.

"She means 'always thinking of ways to make things happen,'" Ruby explained, clueing us in to what the word "resourceful" meant.

"And very smart too," Miss Taylor laughed. "I'm happy to let you all hang in the classroom to work. I will even see if I can bring in a sewing machine."

"Perfect! Together we are unstoppable!" I raised my hand in the air like we'd kicked the winning field goal.

"Speaking of unstoppable," Miss Taylor announced as she stood up, "I'm going to end my lunch break with a walk. Ms. Álvarez is challenging the school staff to a step contest.

44

And I am about to beat my daily goal."

We waved to Miss Taylor as she power walked away from us, and I grinned to myself. Leave it to the Invincible Girls to turn a problem into a super-fun bonding event! I couldn't wait to tell Gammy that I had a way to carry on our family's legacy!

6 THREADY, SET, GO!

People were usually excited for the weekends.

Especially me.

I lived for the weekends.

Nothing but free time for sports and your friends. And Sundays, well, they were the best because Dad would make his amazing breakfasts and we'd settled in to watch football all day long.

This Sunday, though, there wasn't time for football.

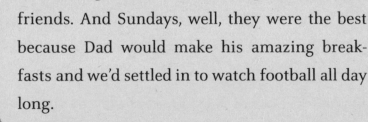

This Sunday my house was filled with all the other Invincible Girls and their families, who had come to share a meal with us. And what a meal it was. Gammy cooked a Sunday dinner that rivaled her Thanksgiving meals, with all my favorite dishes.

Gammy said breaking bread with friends was like sharing a piece of your heart and feeding a part of your soul.

The grown-ups talked and talked. They talked so much before dinner that I didn't know what they'd have to say once we got to the table. The other Invincible Girls and I hung out in the kitchen with Gammy. She taught us how to knead the dough to make her top secret special butter rolls.

"Ms. Gammy, thanks for sharing your baking secrets with us!" Ruby told her. "I don't know if Myka told you or not, but I love to bake."

Gammy laughed. "'Ms. Gammy.' That's awfully formal. You can call me 'Gammy' or 'Ms. Phillips.'

But I prefer 'Gammy.' And I never turn away other cooks from my kitchen!"

"'Gammy' it is, and I'll be back to learn more of your delicious recipes," Ruby said. We joined Gammy around the kitchen table.

"And yes, you girls were a big help. I miss having company while I cook."

Ruby pulled out her notebook and turned all businesslike. "Perfect. Now, I have some questions to ask you."

Gammy sat up straight and folded her flour-covered hands on the table. The honey-butter scent of rolls baking in the oven filled the air between us. "Ask away. I'm an open book." She winked at me.

"What is the difference between a quilt and a regular blanket?" Ruby asked.

"You get straight to the point, don't you!" Gammy laughed. "I asked that same question when I was about your age. And there's a huge difference."

"Really?" Lauren asked. "I had no idea."

"For starters, anyone with money can buy a blanket. Only special people make quilts. Quilts are handmade, stitched with love. Blankets are usually factory-made in bulk. And the making of a quilt is personal and special. It's the start of a legacy," Gammy explained.

"Sort of like the sweaters that my grammy makes!" Ruby said. "Some of the ones I wear are the same ones my mom did!"

"Exactly!" Gammy agreed. "Quilts can be customized to reflect who you are."

"So, are you saying that I could even paint on my squares? Add some art?" Emelyn asked, a flicker of excitement in her eyes.

"Ooooh! That would be really cool!" Lauren said as Gammy nodded.

"Sure. Why not? I think that would be wonderful." Gammy grabbed Emelyn's hand and gave it a squeeze.

"Okay, I have another question," Ruby said.

"Not a problem. Ask away," Gammy told Ruby as she got up to check the rolls.

"How was the quilt given to you?" Ruby paused, and she took a long, deep breath. "I mean, I know your mom passed away when you were younger."

Gammy nodded. "Ruby, you're going to be an amazing reporter. I can feel the empathy and kindness behind your question. Which, by the way, is a great one."

"The Invincible Girls always practice kindness," Ruby said as she beamed at Gammy's compliment.

Gammy hugged her. "My mom was really sick before she passed. While she never got a chance to teach me how to quilt, she gave me our family quilt and told me all about its history. I learned about all six of the women who added to this quilt."

The Invincible Girls hung on to all of Gammy's words, and we leaned toward her, intrigued. Gammy told us the stories her mom had shared with her.

"That's so cool and special that your mom was able to tell you that," Lauren said.

"It totally is," I agreed, loving that I was still learning things about Gammy that I hadn't known.

"Question number three!" Ruby said.

"How many do you have?" Lauren joked.

"I researched the word 'legacy' because it sounds so important, and I didn't want to just throw the word around. Here's what I found: two definitions. One said, 'something given by or received from an ancestor or another person from the past,' and the second said the word means 'a gift given by a will, especially of money or other personal items.' And a will is . . ." Ruby flipped through her notes. "A document that tells others what you want done with your things after you pass away. So, I wonder if you can start a legacy with people who aren't related to you by blood?"

"Great question!" I said.

"I don't see why not," Gammy replied.

"We should create something special," I said.

"We should!" Emelyn agreed.

"An Invincible Girl legacy!" Ruby exclaimed. "Maybe a quilt that celebrates us?"

"Oh, I love that! We are total legacy makers. And one day when we're adults, we can remember how awesome we were as third graders!" I told the group.

Our discussion was interrupted as Dad charged into the kitchen.

"I'm starving. Dinner ready?" he asked. The

rest of the Invincible Girls' parents were right on his heels.

"My dear son-in-love, you're always hungry. That is why I'm feeding the guests first. Everyone, wash your hands and meet me in the dining room." Gammy looked at my friends and me. "Girls, can you do me a favor?"

We nodded.

"Go and get those grandsons of mine so they can help me set the table and serve the food. This food is best when it's hot!"

Gammy winked. Then she pulled the golden-brown buttery rolls out of the oven.

We raced upstairs to get my brothers. Smelling all that good food had my stomach doing an Olympic tumbling routine. We burst into Jordan's room and delivered the message.

I took us on a detour through the living room on the way back, to give the boys enough time to do all the work. Mom and Gammy had hung our family quilt inside a glass frame, and I wanted to

53

show the girls. I was a little sad that I wouldn't be able to hold it anymore, but Gammy said this was how we could preserve it for many decades to come.

"I'm excited to start our quilting classes," Ruby said.

"It's so cool to learn new things. That's how I always feel when I start a new art project," Emelyn agreed. "But the best part is that we're doing this together!"

Ruby rubbed her stomach and turned to

me. "And you know, anytime you want to eat together when your gammy cooks, I'd like to do that too."

We laughed.

I hoped that learning to quilt would be easy. The hard part was done—we'd found a class! I was sure everything else would be smooth sailing.

"Now let's eat before my brothers leave us with the scraps!" I said, and my friends cheered as we made our way to Gammy's Sunday dinner feast.

1 I NEEDLE LITTLE HELP

The four of us spent the entire next day at school watching the clock. Then, when I got home that evening, I rushed through dinner and practically pushed Mom and Gammy out the door. It was go time. Gammy would leave in few weeks, which meant there was no time to waste. We needed to learn the plays, and then practice, if we were going to make beautiful quilts.

The rest of the girls had already arrived at the community center. Emelyn's mom had offered to drive them all and meet us there.

"Do you think we will like Miss Taylor's cousin as much as we like her?" Emelyn asked, clutching her tote bag filled with colorful fabrics.

"I sure hope so," Lauren said as she put her two bags down on a table in the center of the room.

"I do too," someone behind us added.

Our heads whipped around all at once.

We knew that voice!

"Miss Taylor!" we squealed in unison.

"What are you doing here?" Lauren asked.

"Well, you girls are constantly inspiring me. And this time you inspired me to want to learn something new. When I told my cousin you signed up for the class, she pretty much gave me no choice but to come too!"

We hugged Miss Taylor.

"Welcome, everyone!" Our attention was drawn to the woman speaking at the front of the room. She was tall and had oversize green-and-gold glasses. She was wearing a long flowy dress and a crocheted sweater-vest with pockets. Her dark, curly hair was pulled up in two messy buns that had wooden sticks in them. She stood in front of a space that was normally a gym, but it had been transformed into a classroom. There was a projector at the front, and rows of tables.

"Speaking of my cousin," Miss Taylor said, and nodded toward the woman, who was adjusting her headset microphone.

"After you sign in, sit at a table with a sewing machine and supplies and give yourself some space. I'm Krishna Dalal. Welcome to beginners quilting. By the end of our time together, you will have created a bunch of squares to sew together so that you're well on your way to making an original quilt!" she told the group, before tapping her tablet.

The sound of pop dance music filled the air.

"This is my type of class. I feel the art muse

now!" Gammy grabbed my hand, and we started dancing together. "Your mom and I used to dance to this song when she was a little girl. You know, your mom thought she was Whitney Houston," Gammy said. I looked over at Mom, who was unpacking her bag and singing "I Wanna Dance with Somebody" loudly.

"Dance with me, Invincible Girls! And you too, Miss Taylor. I see you peeking. Let's get our creative juices flowing!" Gammy held her hands up and gestured toward us.

The other Invincible Girls put down their stuff and joined Gammy and me for a dance. Emelyn's mom finished setting up our workstations.

Krishna walked over to our dancing circle and joined in. "Great to know that people enjoy my taste in music. I love to bring in good vibes at the start of a class."

"Are those knitting needles in your hair?" Ruby asked.

"Yes, they are. I teach a knitting class next. Do you knit?"

"I do, with my grammy. It's our favorite thing to do."

"I see this is going to be a very creative group right here." Krishna danced with us until the song ended.

"And this is our type of quilting class. I'm Gammy, and this is Lauren, Ruby, Emelyn, and

Myka, also known as the Invincible Girls Club." Gammy smiled.

"Oh, I've heard all about these four from my cousin! Nice to meet you all. The Invincible Girls Club, I love it. Cool squad name!"

Krishna left our dancing circle to go back to the front and turn down the music.

"All right, now that everyone is set up and feeling energized, let's start our Quilting for

Beginners class. Remember, this is about fun, and whatever you make will be beautiful and special because you made it."

"Gammy, that's just what you said," I whispered as I took my seat between her and Mom. The other girls sat at tables in front of me.

Krishna changed the slide on the presentation behind her. The first directions appeared on the screen.

Step One: Turn on your sewing machine.

Step Two: Thread the needle.

I took a deep breath. I really didn't want to screw up in the first two steps! I reread the directions three times for how to prepare the machine. Then I followed the steps, making sure my sewing machine was ready to go. I watched as Ruby threaded the needle. Mom pulled up the directions on her tablet and placed it in front of us.

I looked around the table as everyone took out their beautiful fabrics and prepared to get to work. Even though I knew we were all beginners, it seemed like they all knew what to do.

"You okay, Sweet Pea?" Mom asked. She took the thread from my hands.

"Yes. Just checking the directions again."

There were fifteen of us in class, and we each had our own machine. I looked over at Gammy, and I saw beads of sweat forming on her forehead as she tried to steady her hands to thread the sewing machine needle. She leaned close and squinted as she tried again. She poked around with the thread, but then let out a groan of frustration. Gammy wiped her forehead. She caught me staring. "Myka, please get my reading glasses out of my bag. My eyes aren't as good as they used to be. I can't zoom in on the needle like I zoom in on my text messages."

I laughed, then grabbed Gammy's glasses out of her purse. I watched as she put on the oversize red glasses.

"This is a bit harder than it seems," Gammy

said with her eyebrows furrowed together in full concentration mode.

"Look!" Lauren pulled out her pre-cut squares with dog paw prints all over. "Mom found me this really cool fabric. This reminds me of my love for dogs and the very first thing we did as the Invincible Girls Club."

"That's perfect!" Ruby exclaimed.

"Our conversation with your gammy inspired us," Lauren said to me. "I think we can really make this quilt happen."

"We totally can," Ruby agreed. "Sure, maybe we aren't a blood-related family, but that doesn't mean together we aren't creating a legacy. We're doing awesome things together, so why not create something to unite us?"

"We'll start with sections to represent each of us and then add on to the blank squares in our sections as we continue to do awesome things," Lauren added.

"Which means it might get pretty big!" Ruby said.

"Yeah, and we're hoping that others might see it and be inspired to do great things too," Emelyn added.

"The legacy of the Invincible Girls Club! I love it!" I said.

"We thought you would," Emelyn told me.

Lauren wagged a finger at me. "And don't think for a second that just because you're working on your gammy's quilt, we are going to let you off the hook from adding your section to this one."

"No way! I'm an Invincible Girl, right? I'm adding to the quilt too!" I agreed, a warm, bubbly feeling of happiness fizzing inside me.

"Speaking of working on it . . ." Emelyn gestured toward Krishna, who had begun to talk to the group. The screen behind Krishna clicked to the next slide.

"Follow the directions step by step," Krishna said.

I read the directions.

Step three: Pull out your pre-cut squares. Arrange them on a flat surface. Take a photo of your layout.

Steps one and two complete. By the time the step three directions were on display, I thought making this quilt was going to be a breeze. I reached into the bag to look for our material. We didn't have fancy pre-cut squares from the store. Just my baby blanket and my first soccer jersey, which I now had to cut into squares.

Both Gammy and Mom were busy working on their squares for our quilt. I didn't want to disturb them. I grabbed the sample square from the center of the table to use as my guide. I cut both my soccer jersey and my baby blanket into eight squares each, but the pieces of fabric started to roll up on the sides. They didn't lie flat like the sample square. Everyone else was sewing, and

I was still prepping my squares. I couldn't fall behind, so I took the un-flattened squares and arranged them to be stitched together. Time to get to the sewing machine.

Well, I thought I was ready to go. Krishna said something about starting at a quarter inch.

"Gammy, do I just put my two squares here?"

Gammy nodded, then placed her finger on the one-fourth mark on the metal plate on the sewing machine.

I lined up my squares, placed my foot on the sewing machine pedal, and pushed my fabric under the needle. Then right away, everything started to bunch up. My fabrics weren't smooth and straight like everyone else's. I looked over and saw Lauren, Ruby, and Emelyn all quilting like pros. Even Miss Taylor already had a row of squares all stitched together. Gammy was singing along and quilting. Mom was adding more army fatigue squares with no problem. It was just me who couldn't even stitch in a straight line without bunching the thread.

I yanked my fabric from the machine.

"Be gentle, Sweet Pea," Mom reminded me.

I grabbed two more pieces and tried again. This time I went faster. Same thing. It was all bunched up. I snuck a glance to see if any of the other girls could feel my pain. They were all working hard, and Lauren, who was quilting like she'd skipped JV and been placed on the varsity team, smiled at me. How was it that I was the only one who wasn't getting this?

"Hey, chin up. What did I always tell you? Slow and steady wins the race," Gammy said as she lifted the needle up and pulled the fabric from my sewing machine. "Now grab that seam ripper, and we'll remove this thread and start again."

I picked up the seam ripper and handed it to Gammy. "I guess starting over isn't the worst thing in the world."

"Exactly. Quitting is the worst thing," Gammy confirmed.

"Can I help?" Emelyn asked. "I seem to have gotten the hang of it. Watch me first, and then I'll talk you through it."

Emelyn placed her hands over mine and showed me how to apply just enough pressure that the material didn't bunch up.

"There we go," Emelyn said when it was done. "Sometimes doing things together is the best way to solve a problem!"

I looked at the two pieces of fabric we had joined.

Emelyn was right.

But once she stepped back and I tried again, without her guidance, the pieces bunched.

"No worries!" Emelyn smiled. "We've got this."

"Let's try that again!" I agreed, and the two of us grabbed another square of fabric and set to work together.

8 WHAT'S SEWING ON?

After three weeks of classes, Miss Taylor invited us to stay and work on our quilt squares during recess. If I hadn't been such a team player, I would've bolted out of the class like I'd just been passed the baton at a track meet.

While Emelyn might have helped me out in class that first night, I seemed to forget everything when she wasn't right beside me. Not only that, but at our second class, Krishna announced that we would have a showcase at the end, where

70

we would share our work with everyone. She said it was a highlight of the course, something each group always loved, but there was nothing to love when all I had to share at the moment were sloppy stitches and a few squares that weren't worthy of hanging on anyone's wall.

We'd had six classes now, and by the looks of the other Invincible Girls' bags, I was the only one who wasn't progressing. My quilt was small, with only a few squares joined. Lauren, Emelyn, and Ruby had bags stuffed with what looked like a million squares sewn together.

"Myka, are you okay?" Emelyn asked after the class had emptied. She had big heart earrings in her ears that dangled down, and I focused on those instead of looking into her eyes.

I shrugged. "I'm okay."

"You don't seem like it," Lauren said.

"Yeah, as a matter of fact, I noticed that you haven't been the same since we started quilting lessons," Ruby added.

"I'll figure it out." I cleared off my desk to make room for my quilt. But I didn't need much space, because while I'd made a small section for the Invincible Girls Club quilt, I'd only managed to sew four squares for my family quilt.

Miss Taylor walked back into the room pushing a cart of sewing machines. "I'm so excited we could do this. I don't know about you girls, but that quilting class flies by, and at home I barely have time to marathon my favorite shows, let alone work on my new hobby." Miss Taylor took the sewing machines off the cart and placed them on desks near outlets. "I had to promise Krishna that I'd bring her over a batch of my granola, but I think that is well worth it to borrow these. Lucky for us that the community center still had these old ones in storage."

"Oh wow, that's cool," Lauren said.

"This is perfect. I wanted more time to work on my quilt. I'm glad we can do this together," Ruby said.

I sank into my seat as I watched Lauren dump out some squares and other fabric items for her quilt. I glanced over at Emelyn, who was arranging her quilt on the small-group table. Ruby spread out some embroidery and other embellishments.

"My mom took me shopping to get some cool embroidered fabrics for us to add to our quilt. This way they'll really show our personalities. Miss Taylor, you can have some too," Ruby offered.

I stayed in my seat as they all went over to grab the beaded and bejeweled material. No amount of fancy polyester and cotton was going to make me a better quilter.

"This is fantastic, Ruby. Girls, your squares look amazing. I can't believe you're novice quilters," Miss Taylor gushed.

"What's a novice?" Lauren asked.

"It means 'a beginner.' If you ask me, you all are experts," Miss Taylor said.

I felt far from an expert as I flicked on the power switch. But the sewing machine didn't turn on.

I waved my hand to get Miss Taylor's attention. "My sewing machine isn't working. Maybe I'll just watch you sew."

Miss Taylor came over to me. "Let me see."

She tried several sockets until she finally plugged the cord into a socket that made all the lights on the machine come on.

"There. I think I'd better put in a request to

get these outlets fixed," Miss Taylor said.

I slowly took out my small quilt. Even Lauren's quilt was larger despite her missing the Wednesday classes.

"Myka, we can tell something is bothering you," Emelyn said. "Let us help."

Miss Taylor sat next to me. "How can we turn Myka's frown upside down?"

"My quilt really isn't a quilt at all. I'm nowhere near as far as you all are." I told the other Invincible Girls and Miss Taylor how I felt discouraged, how it felt like they were all hitting home runs and I couldn't even get past first base.

"I'm following directions. I'm not skipping any steps, but it is still taking me too long. And when I try to up my speed, everything gets messed up."

"But, Myka, sometimes it's okay that you're not moving as fast as everyone else," Emelyn said.

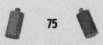

"I know you may disagree, but everything isn't a race," Lauren added.

My shoulders slumped. "Try telling that to my brothers. Everything is a competition. They're going to tease me."

"I'm sure they won't tease you," Miss Taylor said.

"Miss Taylor, my brothers dream about creative ways to tease me," I explained.

"I think that's in the brother's handbook. Job one, tease your sister," Lauren told me, and laughed. "The stepbrother's handbook too."

"Well, they can't tease you if you don't quit," Ruby said.

"She's right. All that matters is that you keep trying." Miss Taylor handed me my next square, which was white with blue stripes cut from my first baseball jersey. Gammy had bought it for me when I'd still been a bun in Mom's oven.

I took the square and lined it up to be added to another square. Emelyn, Lauren, and Ruby looked at me with big encouraging *You can do it* eyes. I placed my foot on the pedal and slowly stitched the squares together. Everything was in a perfect line, nice and straight. The girls cheered.

"See. You've got this!" Miss Taylor said. "Let's get to work, girls."

"I can't wait for the showcase!" Lauren told us as she cut a piece of fabric.

My stomach dropped. That was the last thing I wanted to think about.

"Not just because we get to share our work but because I have a surprise about it," she added.

"A surprise?" I asked Lauren.

"Yep! I suggested to Krishna the idea that we could invite our families to come! She totally dug it and agreed!"

"What a great idea!" Ruby said at the same time my mind spun with reasons why I didn't want my family there. Now things were even worse!

Time was going by so fast, but my quilting skills moved like a snail.

There was only one more class before the showcase.

The time crunch meant that I had to deliver. I had to make sure Gammy and I created the quilt she deserved. This was the fourth quarter of the soccer game.

It was time for me to score some goals.

LAST-STITCH EFFORT

Unfortunately, sometimes when you go to kick a goal, the ball sails high over the net instead. Or, in my actual case, I didn't get better at quilting.

"Is it possible to get worse at something you're learning?" I asked Mom as she drove Gammy and me home from quilting class.

The *last* class before the showcase.

Mom glanced at me in the rearview mirror before returning her gaze to the road. "You're not getting worse, honey. Some things are harder to learn than others. Which is why I always say that practice makes progress."

"I thought practice made perfect," I told her.

Mom laughed. "That just sounds better, but in reality you're making progress."

That was what made Mom so great. I didn't have to tell her what was wrong. She just knew. And what to say to make it better.

"I've been learning for a really long time," I said quietly, but before Mom or Gammy could respond, we were home.

The moment she turned the car off, I made a mad dash to my bedroom. I didn't slow down or stop to speak with Dad or my brothers. My greetings were tossed into the air on my way upstairs. I heard Jordan's whispered voice behind me talking to Gammy. I heard her say my name, but I didn't wait around to hear her response. And I didn't want anyone to give me their pity because I was the baby of the family. I couldn't stop walking because if I had, I would have started crying.

I just didn't know what to do. I'd never felt like this. When I played sports, I could practice hard. Run more drills or do more exercises to increase my skills or stamina. With quilting there was a flow and a rhythm. I was just not getting it. And the worst part was that I didn't understand why. But now I'd let everyone down because I couldn't learn fast enough. I couldn't face Gammy. Not while the tears were so close to sliding down my cheeks. I plopped onto my bed like doing a belly flop into the pool. I squeezed my eyes shut and quickly fell asleep.

Gammy stood over me as I blinked, waking up from my nap. My eyes couldn't quite focus on Gammy; the lamp shined brightly behind her, making her look like she was getting superpowers.

"Great. You're awake."

"I can't believe I slept that long. Is it past midnight?"

"No." Gammy laughed. "You only snoozed for

about an hour. Come downstairs. I've got something to show you."

Gammy put out her hand, and I grabbed hold of it. Together we walked downstairs.

I didn't smell anything cooking, so she wasn't planning to cheer me up with food. I hoped we didn't have a Bader Family Talk It Out Meeting. At the bottom of the steps, Gammy turned to me.

"Cover your eyes, please," she said in a quiet voice.

I placed the palms of my hands over my eyes, and Gammy guided me down from the steps and into one of the downstairs rooms.

"Okay, Sweet Pea, open them," Gammy said.

When I opened my eyes, I saw that the dining room table had been transformed into a sewing station.

I looked at Jordan, Remy, Alex, and Dad, all standing on either side of Mom behind an old-looking sewing machine.

"What's all this?" I asked.

"This is the Bader family sticking together," Mom said. "You know our motto, 'Never leave family behind.'"

"That's right," Alex agreed. "Well, unless it's Remy and he hasn't showered."

"Your brothers and I heard about your quilting struggles, and we want to help," Dad added. "We asked Mom and Gammy to teach us so we can make sure you finish your squares."

I looked to Gammy, then to my parents and my brothers. "This is amazing. And I was worried that Remy, Alex, and Jordan were going to tease me because I couldn't do it."

Remy walked over and put his arm around my shoulders. "Nah, we only tease about silly stuff. This is important. We're family, and this is our legacy too."

Gammy turned to me. "Now, your friend Ruby called and told us you've been struggling during your recess sewing sessions. Maybe if you used this vintage sewing machine that belonged to my mother, you'd have more success. It's not as up-to-date and modern like the one in school or at quilting class. There's not a lot of bells and whistles, but it works. It still sews."

I smiled and sat down in front of the beige-and-yellow machine, imagining my great-grandmother learning how to quilt on this very machine. "I'm ready, Gammy."

Gammy handed me a folded quilt that was too big to be mine, but I saw my squares. "You fixed it?"

"Not exactly. We added the squares where you messed up. Mistakcs are how we learn. No one is expecting perfection," Mom said. "We added our fabric to yours. Uniting the individual squares is what will make our family quilt complete."

"We fail or succeed together," Jordan said. "And since your friends helped you sharpen your skills, your family is going to help you complete

85

the mission." He placed his arm around me and pulled me in for a hug. Well, it was more of a squeeze and release—Jordan wasn't super affectionate.

"That's right!" Alex said. "Mom and Gammy showed us how to cut out squares using clothing and other material that were important to us. You know, stuff we wanted to pass down."

"Dad did most of the sewing," admitted Remy.

"I haven't had much time to learn, but I'm doing my best," Dad said.

I smiled a smile so bright, it could've lit up New York City. "You guys are the best!"

It felt as if my family's love had just activated strength I hadn't known was in me. But there was also this part of me that felt like I was about to try to dribble the soccer ball across the field after a rainstorm. Any moment now, I'd slip and fall before scoring the goal.

"What do you say, Myka? We get this quilt ready for the showcase as a family?" Mom smiled.

I thought quilting with Gammy and Mom had been cool, but now that my whole family was down—even my brothers, who never did anything not related to sports—it made this quilting experience epic. It no longer mattered if my squares weren't perfect or neat—this was just a moment I'd never forget. "Let's do this!"

"Myka, will you do the honors and bring this family quilt into the end zone?" Dad asked.

Gammy and Mom lined up the remaining pieces. Dad, Jordan, Alex, and Remy stood across the table, each holding a pair of scissors in their hand. We were going to finish this together.

"Let's go, Myka!" Remy cheered.

"Oh, I like that. Say it again," Gammy said.

My brothers put down their scissors and encouraged me. "Let's go, Myka!"

CLAP, CLAP, CLAP, CLAP, CLAP.

"I'm ready," I said.

With Gammy's hand guiding me and my confidence on ten after the other Invincible Girls' help, I stitched practically perfect lines. No fabric buckling or jumbled thread. Maybe practice had made perfect, or maybe it was because I was finishing the quilt with my family, but I no longer worried about the showcase. Everything was going to be just fine.

We did it!

We finished the family quilt!

And together we continued our legacy and created a new one.

We sat around the dining room table way past my bedtime, admiring our hard work. The quilt was big enough to use on a twin-size bed. We sang all our favorite songs, ate popcorn with hot sauce and garlic butter—the Gammy special—and talked about how we would share the quilt among the seven of us. I looked up at Gammy's family quilt framed in the other room and imagined that one day this quilt would be just as special.

ALL PATCHED UP

It's crazy how different things can be when you have a team on your side.

Instead of the dread that had been in the pit of my stomach for so long, I couldn't wait to share my quilt.

So, on our final day of class, when we were set to present, I didn't walk into the community center.

I strutted.

The Bader family quilt was folded up in a

duffel bag. A quilt that was now big enough to cover my bed, with a little extra room to cuddle under. I proudly removed my quilt from the bag.

And on either side of me was my family. My parents, brothers, and Gammy. Our group entered just as we had worked on the quilt— together.

The community center was already full of people laughing, talking, and walking around to check out the quilts laid out on the tables we had worked on during class. Krishna had added her special touch with garlands made of scrap fabric tied around rope, and a banner that read WELCOME in a hodgepodge of fabrics she had cut out and sewn.

Dad grinned at me. "You girls thought this up?"

"It was Lauren's idea! To invite our families," I said. "You know, like with sports. You can only practice so much until it's game time and you want to show the world your skills!"

"Or wow them, if your skills are anything like mine!" Jordan joked, and pretended to shoot a basketball.

Dad pulled me toward him and gave my finger a squeeze. "Just when I think the Invincible Girls Club has accomplished so much, you surprise us with another amazing thing!"

"Hey, Myka! Over here!" Ruby yelled, and waved from across the room. She was standing by a table full of cupcakes, no doubt from Sprinkle & Shine.

"Sugar! Now, that's what I'm talking about!" Remy cheered as he made a beeline straight to the sweets.

I made my way over too, but before I could get far, Krishna turned off the music and the room went silent.

"Hello and welcome!" she began. The bangles on her arms clinked together as she waved to us. "If you could take a seat, we'll get started. I know I have some very talented quilters who

91

want to share what they've been up to these last four weeks."

My brothers made it a point to take the seats right by the snack table.

"Just in case," Remy told me with a wink.

I sat next to Gammy and cozied up against her. She snuck a kiss onto my forehead in response.

"I'm so proud of you," she whispered into my ear.

When everyone was seated, Krishna smiled. "I'm excited to have you all here. While I've been teaching this class for over ten years, never have I had a more enthusiastic group, or one with such a great idea as inviting their families and friends to see the magic that they've stitched up!"

I wiggled in excitement. I couldn't wait to present my quilt and our family's legacy.

One by one, each member of the class shared their creation and the meaning of the squares that they'd chosen.

Miss Taylor had gotten a ton of her quilt done. It was full of gorgeous jewel-toned colors that she said were the colors of the birthstones for everyone in her family.

"It's the perfect quilt to cozy up under and grade papers!" she said, and winked at us girls.

I raised my hand to go next, and my family cheered as I walked to the front of the room. Their enthusiasm and love wrapped around me like the fabric of my quilt would.

I held the quilt up to the group and took a deep breath. It was like being in Miss Taylor's room all over again and sharing personal information. But I could do it. No, wait. I *wanted* to do it.

"I didn't make this quilt," I told the group, and paused. "*We* made the quilt. The Bader family. And every single piece of it was stitched together with love. So get on up here, everyone! We all need to share!"

I gestured to my family to come up and join

me. As they made their way toward me, I continued to talk. "These are the people who blanket me with love over and over again. Their encouragement and support is never-ending, which is why this quilt is so special to me. We made it together, and it represents our family bond."

Gammy put her hand on my shoulder and gave it a squeeze, and I talked directly to her. "I'm proud we could continue our family's legacy."

"I am too," she replied, and her eyes sparkled with tears.

I opened my arms to all of them to welcome a giant Bader family group hug. The kind that squeezed the breath out of you in a whoosh. The kind that reminded you of how important family was.

"Wow!" Krishna said after a few more members of our class had presented. "What a creative group!"

"Wait until you see our quilt!" Ruby interrupted. "It's the pièce de résistance."

"The what?" Lauren asked, her forehead scrunched up as she looked at Ruby, confused.

"It's French. It means 'the focus of the night'! The masterpiece! Our quilt!" Ruby clarified.

Krishna laughed. "Well, that's certainly one way to introduce your project."

"It's totally worth the buildup," Ruby promised as the rest of us went up front with her. We each had completed our own section, and the plan was to hold them next to each other to show the room what the finished product would look like when they were sewn together. Emelyn had all our squares in her bag.

But instead of our individual squares, Emelyn pulled out a giant piece of fabric.

"Our sections are a quilt!" I squealed in delight.

"We stitched them together!" Lauren told me as she nodded at Emelyn's mom. "Well, with a little bit of help."

"We wanted it to be a surprise," Emelyn

added. "You were working so hard on your family's quilt, we wanted to do something special for you."

"And not only that. We added some more squares using pieces of fabric that are meaningful to all of us together," Ruby said.

Krishna wrapped up the formal part of the showcase and welcomed everyone to view the quilts and eat some snacks.

I spread out the Invincible Girls Club quilt and examined it closer.

"It's perfect," I told my friends.

"Perfectly us!" Ruby said.

"Yep, see, there's some from one of the dog shelter shirts." Lauren pointed to the square that said *Paws for Reading*.

"And the shirt I wore when we painted the mural on the wall of the school," Emelyn said.

"And the flannel shirt my dad wore when we went camping!" Ruby added.

"Just like we talked about at the start," I told

them. "The legacy we will leave as Invincible Girls."

I smiled at all the memories this quilt held for us.

"This quilt is a fabulous idea," Krishna told us as she walked over to the group. "And so clever!"

"One of the things we learned during our classes is that family doesn't have to be related by blood," Lauren said. "Our club is a little family too!"

"A little family of awesomeness!" Ruby added.

"I consider all of you my sisters," I agreed.

"And guess what the best part is!" Lauren exclaimed. "We didn't make the quilt for us. Nope. The Invincible Girls are all about sharing and connecting with others. We already talked to Ms. Rez at school, and she would love to hang it in the library."

"Yep! Like our team flag!" Ruby added.

I sucked in a breath. "That would be perfect!"

Our school library was magical, thanks to Ms. Rez, who covered it in bright, colorful items that celebrated and welcomed everyone. It was a place where you wanted to stay forever, and there was no doubt our quilt would fit right in.

"She also promised that if anyone asked about the quilt, she'd tell them all about our club," Ruby said. "Who knows, maybe it will inspire millions to be a part of the club!"

I laughed. Ruby always did dream big. But then again, what was better than reaching for the impossible?

"Or it might at least inspire others to make the world a better place," Emelyn added, always making things a bit more attainable.

"And when they do, they can keep adding brand-new sections with us!" Lauren added.

I ran my fingers over the squares and couldn't believe what we had created.

"You three are the best," I told them.

"Nope, that's where you're wrong," Ruby

said with a grin. "The *four* of us are the best!"

"We're invincible!" Lauren added.

And in that moment, I realized I didn't need a quilt to keep me warm.

Nope.

The love of my family and friends would always blanket me with love and warm my heart up.

11 BLANKETED IN LOVE

I wished that Gammy could stay with us forever. Her visits always felt too short. But right after our quilt presentations, Gammy let us know that she was about to hit the road *again*. This time she was going on an eleven-day cruise around the Mediterranean.

"Mom, I think you could write me a note for school to explain that I went with Gammy. Miss Taylor would understand. And I could bring back gifts for my brothers and the other Invincible

Girls," I joked, my arm wrapped around Gammy. My head pressed against her soft fleece jacket in hopes that she'd feel guilty for leaving me behind and make Mom let me go with her.

"Myka, we went over this. You can't miss school to travel the world with Gammy," Mom said.

Gammy kissed my forehead and gave me a squeeze. No luck. Gammy agreed with Mom.

"Even when I'm away, my love will always cover you. Remember that," she said.

Gammy always said that, but I wished she'd just stay or take me with her.

My shoulders slumped and I plopped onto the couch.

"Is there anything else you need the boys to bring downstairs?" Dad asked as he shouldered Gammy's duffel bags.

"Nope. That's it. Everything else I am leaving for Myka and the boys. You take good care of our quilt and our family sewing machine."

"You got it, Gammy," I agreed.

Remy, Alex, and Jordan helped Dad take her heavy bags to the car. Gammy grabbed my hand and led me into the kitchen.

"You ready for one last secret?" Gammy asked.

My eyes lit up, and my heart raced with excitement. "You know I am."

Gammy pulled a small box out of her purse. A mini box with flowers and hearts all over it. One that looked like it held large index cards.

"These are our family recipes. I placed all your favorite Gammy meals in the front." Gammy opened the top of the box. "I'm passing this on to you."

I stretched my hands out for the box, afraid that I might drop it. It was almost as if I could smell scents of the different meals coming from the box. In my hands I held the key to making all our family's soul-food Sunday dinners.

"How come you never gave this to Mom?" I asked.

Gammy gave me a look. "You know cooking is not your mom's specialty."

"True," I said.

"Everyone knows your dad is the chef in this family. But don't tell him I said so." Gammy laughed.

"Okay, I'll keep your secret. But I'm not a chef either," I told her.

Gammy pinched my cheek. "Not yet, and you may never be. But I know that you will make sure that the right person gets this next."

"The right person?" I asked.

"Yep, I can't quite put my finger on it, but I know you can decide which one of your brothers to give this to first. One of them will be our next family chef. I am trusting you with the honor of passing it along. From one only girl to the next." Gammy winked. "It was my older brother who taught me how to cook."

After the way my whole family had come together and made our quilt, I knew we could make Gammy's recipes together as well. And something told me that as much as Remy liked to eat, he might be the next Bader chef.

I pulled out the paper stuck in the front.

"What's this?" I asked.

"A special note for you. And I'd like you to share it with your friends."

I looked down at the note card and read the note out loud.

"Eat good food. Love your family and friends. And be invincible!"

Gammy wrapped her arms around me and led me out of the kitchen toward the rest of the family in the car.

And that was exactly what the other Invincible Girls and I were going to do. As Gammy and I walked to the car, I thought, *This is just the beginning. Our legacy continues.*

Hello, Amazing Reader!

If you're a member of the Invincible Girls Club, then welcome back! And, well, if you're new to the family like me and this is your first time kicking it with Myka, Ruby, Lauren, and Emelyn, I'm so hyped that you're here!

The four girls are just as passionate about making a difference as they are about loving their families and their friends. I hope that they inspire you to want to capture the legacy of your family, school, and community. Everyone has a special place in the world.

You don't have to be an adult to start your legacy or leave an impact!

Everyone has a story that makes them unique.

Everyone has the potential to be great and leave a mark on this world, no matter how big or small.

Everyone can be invincible.

So, if you haven't become a member, then join me on this awesome adventure. This is your official invitation to show the world that there isn't only one way to leave your mark on the world. We need every girl; we are stronger together. All girls joined as one makes the fabric of our quilt that much stronger.

Love,

Steph B. Jones

aka . . . the newest recruit to the Invincible Girls Club

MEET
INVINCIBLE GIRL
Emma Watson

Emma is an actress from the United Kingdom (she played Hermione in the Harry Potter films!) and a huge champion for girls and women everywhere. She speaks out about girls' right to education and the importance of women having the same opportunities as men, and celebrates

 107

amazing women and girls so the world knows their names! She is a UN Women Goodwill Ambassador for Great Britain and helped launch HeForShe in her country. HeForShe is an organization that encourages both men and women to work together to make sure everyone is treated equally. Emma is an Invincible Girl because she works nonstop to empower women and inspire them to use their talents to shine.

MEET
INVINCIBLE GIRL
Joy Lindsay

Joy used her creative talents to write a children's book called *When a Butterfly Chooses to Fly* as a tribute to a sister who had passed away. Joy shared this book with students and realized that many of the young women had their own unique voices and stories to tell. She was inspired to create the nonprofit Butterfly Dreamz, which works to empower girls through mentorships, scholarships, leadership training, exposure to opportunities and careers, classes on writing, and the opportunity to publish so that all girls can get their words out. Joy is an Invincible Girl because she's providing the tools for a future generation of girls to change the world.

MEET
INVINCIBLE GIRL
Alexandra Scott

Alex wasn't even a year old when she was first diagnosed with cancer. Although she appeared to beat the cancer at first, it came back multiple times. When she was four, she decided that she wanted to raise money to help find a cure for cancer. Determined to make a difference, she raised over $2000 with her first lemonade stand! Ignited by her success, Alex and her family continued to raise money to help fund research for childhood cancer by having lemonade stands (even when she was sick and in and out of the hospital). She raised over a million dollars before she passed away when she was eight. Alex was an Invincible Girl because even when sick, she worked to make the lives of other children with forms of pediatric cancer better in the future.

MEET
INVINCIBLE GIRL
Beyoncé Knowles

Beyoncé is legendary. Since the age of sixteen, in her stilettos, she's used her remarkable talents to quilt together a legacy that is like none other. She's a singer, actress, songwriter, businesswoman, humanitarian, and visionary. One of Beyoncé's biggest legacies is her BeyGOOD Foundation.

Through this organization, she has provided hundreds of thousands of dollars to aid the fight for global gender equality, given school supplies to students across the country, and hosted food drives and disaster relief. Much of the success she's earned and money she has made has been used to pay it forward, enriching the lives of others. As the first Black woman to headline the music festival Coachella, she not only used her moment to pay homage to and shine a light on the significant legacy of historically Black colleges and universities (HBCUs). Along with her husband, Jay-Z (Shawn Carter), she partnered with Tiffany & Co. to launch the About Love campaign, through which they will donate millions of dollars in HBCU scholarships. Beyoncé is an Invincible Girl because her legacy is far reaching, and she's dedicated to ensuring that Invincible Girls will continue to run the world.

MEET
INVINCIBLE GIRL
Jayna Zweiman

Jayna is a multi-genre artist who has turned her skills and love of making things into a way to change the world for the better. She's created whole movements around the power of creating items (hats, masks, and blankets) to connect people and causes. One of her current projects,

Welcome Blanket, invites those who knit, crochet, quilt, weave, or sew to create a blanket that is given to a refugee family as they arrive in America. Each blanket includes a handwritten note of welcome and an immigration story important to the blanket creator's family. There have been over six thousand blankets gifted to new families, and the project has been described as a way to craft the society she believes we have the potential to be, stitch by stitch. Jayna is an Invincible Girl because she uses her art to create items that remind every single person of how important they are and that they matter in this world.

★ MEET
INVINCIBLE GIRL ★
Malala Yousafzai

Malala is a champion of girls' fight for equal education and the opportunity to go to school. She was born in Pakistan and loved school. However, she was forced to leave school when she was eleven, after the Taliban took control of her town and banned girls from getting an education.

 117

Malala chose to speak out about the unfairness of this, and by doing so, she became a target of the Taliban. Because she stood up for her beliefs and rights, Malala was shot, but that did not stop her. After her recovery, she continued to advocate for the right of all girls to attend school, and she speaks out against those who work to prohibit that. She helped to create Malala Fund, which is "working for a world where every girl can learn and lead." She is the youngest person to ever be awarded the Nobel Peace Prize and continues to empower girls. Malala is an Invincible Girl because she's a tireless champion for girls and women all over the world whose right to an education is denied.

INVINCIBLE GIRL

Olga Segura

Olga was born in Mexico, and much of the work she does helps to promote, empower, and celebrate her heritage. She used her background as an actress to start her own production company with her brother and a fellow actor, she helped create the Latinx House, and she is a cofounder of Decididas. All of these are platforms to help the Latinx community communicate with one another and get their voices heard in film and art. She also helped found Los Ángeles en México, which is a program of One Children's Foundation. It works to improve the lives of children in impoverished communities and countries by providing them with food, shelter, and education. Olga is an Invincible Girl because of her deep love for her Mexican heritage and her desire to provide resources to help others from her country and beyond.

MEET
INVINCIBLE GIRL
Michelle Obama

Former First Lady Michelle Obama is invincible through and through, and the legacy she leaves will affect many generations to come. While acting as First Lady at the White House, she worked to change the lifestyles of families everywhere by inspiring them to make movement and healthy eating not only a priority but fun too. Her Let's Move! program worked with community members, schools, and faith leaders to make health programs and fresh foods accessible to people everywhere. She also headed up the Reach Higher initiative, which helped to show students the importance of completing education beyond high school and informed them of the opportunities and programs available. She also encouraged girls all over the globe and showed them the power of an education. Michelle Obama is an Invincible Girl because she has worked endlessly to better the lives and futures of so many.

MEET INVINCIBLE GIRL
Dolly Parton

Dolly is like a quilt herself. She's made up of many amazing parts and pieces. She's part singer, part songwriter, part actress, part humanitarian, and so many other things. She even wrote a song about the jacket her mom made her out of fabric pieces when she was a child—her own quilt to wear! She's best known for her long musical career, and much of the money she has made from that success has been used to enrich the lives of others. One of Dolly's biggest legacies is the Imagination Library, a nonprofit she started as a tribute to her dad, who couldn't read. She began it by donating books to children near where she grew up, but now, almost thirty years later, the library has expanded worldwide and she gives over a million books a month to children! Dolly is an Invincible Girl because she has used her talents and gifts to give back to others, so that children everywhere can be wrapped in the love and magic of books and the worlds introduced within the pages.

INVINCIBLE GIRL

Reshma Saujani

Reshma entered the workforce as a lawyer and then ran for Congress. It was during her campaign run, as she toured schools, that she changed course. She saw how few girls were taking computing classes, and she wanted to change that. She started the nonprofit Girls Who

Code (GWC). The mission of the organization is to increase the number of women who work in computer technology. GWC does this by offering outreach, training, support, and resources to girls at a young age. The organization provides opportunities for girls to try out and learn skills for jobs that are usually done by males. Reshma's hope is that girls see the power and talent within themselves and their ability to pursue a life in coding, and Girls Who Code helps make that happen. Reshma is an Invincible Girl because she is working to change the world of programming by filling it with women.

MEET
INVINCIBLE GIRL
Nancy Gianni

Shortly after Nancy's daughter GiGi was born, the doctor diagnosed GiGi with Down syndrome. This is a condition that causes delays in development, including one's ability to reason and remember. Nancy didn't want her daughter to be treated differently, so she vowed to change the way others looked at GiGi and others with Down syndrome. Nancy created the nonprofit GiGi's Playhouse as a place where children diagnosed with Down syndrome and their families could go for resources and networking. Through the programs at GiGi's Playhouse, the children grow more confident, practice important physical and social skills, and attend events that focus on the entire family. Nancy is an Invincible Girl because she's created over fifty places where kids with Down syndrome can go to spend time with peers and increase their skills in lots of different areas.

MEET
INVINCIBLE GIRL
Marley Dias

Marley is living proof that you can make a difference at any age! She started a campaign called 1000 Black Girl Books. When she was in elementary school, she was inspired to make a difference when she couldn't find many books with Black female main characters. She made

129

a goal to find a thousand such books. However, when others heard about what she was doing, the campaign grew into a major movement! She has now collected over thirteen thousand books and has no plans of stopping! Marley has won numerous awards for the change she's making, has written a book showing how other kids can make change too, and is executive producer and host of a Netflix series celebrating Black authors. Marley is an Invincible Girl because she is working to change classrooms, libraries, and homes everywhere so that Black female characters are represented on all bookshelves.

MEET
INVINCIBLE GIRL
Liz Ferro

Liz has been running since she was young. She first used it as a form of therapy and found that the more she ran, the better she felt, both physically and mentally. She has run in over seventy-five marathons, including one in each of the fifty US states! Liz knew that running could help others too, which inspired her to start Girls with Sole. It's a nonprofit whose mission is to use free fitness and wellness programs to empower the minds, bodies, and souls of girls in the greater Cleveland area who are at risk or experienced abuse. The organization focuses on outreach to girls who lack support in other areas of their lives. The program gives the girls everything they need to run: instruction, space, time, guidance, and equipment (such as shoes and water bottles). Liz is an Invincible Girl because she's giving girls the tools they need for a lifetime of fitness, empowerment, and well-being.

Ways That You Can Be an Invincible Girl and Leave a Legacy!

- Create your own quilt to teach others about yourself! This could be done in a traditional way (sewing fabric) or in other creative ways (colored squares of paper, photos, a painted mural of squares). Create one with your family, friends, or school.

- Talk to different family members and capture their stories. You can write them down or record them as audio or video, then create a scrapbook or a quilt of your own!

- Start capturing YOUR stories to pass on and share with others. Keep a journal, diary, sketchbook, or photo album to record your life. No moment is too small!

- Create a time capsule with your family members or friends, full of things that are meaningful and important to all of you. Plan to open it together on a future date. (It's always fun to pick a date ten, twenty, or even thirty years in the future!)
- Start a tradition! It could be something simple, like a weekly game night or ice cream for dinner on the day before a new school year starts—or something bigger, like each year everyone who is at Thanksgiving dinner signs their name on a tablecloth, or celebrate the welcoming of each new baby in the family by knitting a blanket.
- Make it a point to read books that feature characters from backgrounds different from your own. If it's a book that was bought, consider placing it in a Little Free Library near you when you're done, so others can discover it too!

- Start your own book drive for your school, collecting books featuring diverse characters to fill the shelves.
- Take day trips with your family to explore new places that relate to your family's background and/or culture (restaurants, museums, landmarks).
- Investigate your family history. See how far back you can trace your family's genealogy, and create a family tree representing it all.
- Family walks are a great way to learn about your family and have conversations! Make it a routine to go on a walk after dinner each night or every Sunday morning. (You pick the time and frequency.) Leave your devices at home and simply connect through conversation. You'll be surprised at all the great talks you'll have!
- Have a cultural day at school or in your neighborhood. Share your background, culture, beliefs,

and customs with others. Celebrate what makes everyone different and amazing!

• What are traditional foods from your family's culture? Try making one of them!

• Learning about your family's stories from different points of view is a fun thing to do! Consider important life events (births, birthdays, weddings, firsts), then ask different family members or friends for their version of the same event!

• Create a happiness/warm-fuzzy jar or box! Find a large jar (it doesn't need to be fancy; it could even be something you recycle), and at the end of each day write down on a tiny slip of paper one good thing that happened. Fold it up and put it in the jar. Invite your family members to do the same. Watch the slips of paper full of good things grow and grow! Go back at the end of the year and read all the slips or choose some to read whenever you're having a bad day, to remind you of all the happiness in your world!

- Write a letter to your future self on each birthday. Reflect on the past year and then add your hopes for the future. Open that letter one year later, and then continue to write new ones for the years to come to continue this cycle.

- Collect your own family recipes and place them into a book or computer document. For fun, try to make the recipes yourself with adult supervision! You could even put your unique spin on them to add a little bit of yourself to the recipe!

- Teach your friends or family something new that you're good at. What can you do well that you are able to share? Pass your talents on!

- Volunteer! Share your time and talent with others. It will inspire you and help them! Even better, volunteer with your family and make it a tradition!

- Learn about and celebrate your culture by using the arts! Watch movies, listen to music, and explore artists from your culture—or new cultures! It's fun to learn about the cultures of others!

- Have an annual Family Celebration Day, where you create certificates to reward and recognize family members in a ceremony for all the awesome things they accomplished in the previous year!

Acknowledgments

Pardon me while I pinch myself. I can't believe this is real. First, I've been blessed to live a life filled with Invincible Girls.

I can't thank enough the Invincible Girls who are still with me and those who are no longer with me, for inspiring me to dream beyond what was expected from a Black girl from Newark, New Jersey. So many of us don't even realize our capacity or invincibility. Take it from me, you can do all things.

You ARE doing amazing things.

I see you.

A very special thank-you to all the Invincible Girls in my family, those who have inspired me and continue to inspire me . . . my mom (Michelle), and my nanny (Elizabeth) and grandma (Rochelle), who were my very own Gammy in the flesh. My one and only sister (Shareé), my aunts who watch over me from heaven (Mary, Rosie, and Mackcine), and those still with me (Tommysena, Cheryl, Allison, and Lori), my mom-n-love (Ella Mae), my sisters-n-love (Monfia, Jasmine, and Treacy), my cousins (Kaleemah, Khierstan, Tiffany, Cassandra, Connie, Amber, Shawnea, Donya, Melissa, Amirah, Danielle, Khalilah, Jennifer), my nieces (Autumn, Asia, Aaryn, Jayla, Ava, Eboni, Eileyiah, Tierra, Chelsea, and Nyla), and the two pieces of my heart that live outside of my body, my daughters, Mia and Laila. You push Mommy beyond her limits because in your eyes, there are no ceilings.

Thank you to my favorite group of Invincible Girls, who are teachers. You inspire me to be a better educator, pushing me past my comfort zone, reminding me why *we* were called to this work. Charity Haygood, Yasmeen Sampson, Danielle Mastrogiovanni, Dollister Baker, Doretta Sockwell, Genique Flournoy-Hamilton, Kena Culver, Lisa Fischman, Nicole Johnson, Nykita Dixon, Monique Grady, Monique Lynch, Santa Tillis, Shanell

Rodriguez-Johnson, Terri Cohen, Tina Ehsanipour, Wanda Davis, Wendy Davidson, and Yasmin McClinton.

An Invincible Girl is nothing without her best friends. I've known these Invincible Girls for longer than I can remember, and they're more than friends; they're my sisters no matter what. Thank you, Leah, Kelly, Sameerah, and Tamika.

Thank you to the Invincible Girls who came to me as educators at varying points in my academic journey and poured their knowledge and wisdom into me: Mrs. Lonon, Ms. Bishop, Mrs. Hatcher, Ms. Hewitt, and Dr. Mia Zamora.

Thank you to the group of Invincible Girls who have been creating a legacy like none other since 1908. The illustrious women of Alpha Kappa Alpha Sorority, Incorporated, a sisterhood of women who believe in promoting unity and friendship among women and providing service to all mankind. A sisterhood I am proud to have the privilege to be a part of thanks to my mentor, my auntie, my sorority sister, Cheri Phillips. Thank you to my Beta Alpha Omega sisters and my LS, Eight Is Enough—we started this journey together.

Thank you to all my fellow writers who are Invincible Girls, because not only are they breaking down walls and barriers with their own stories but they reach back and pull other girls up who look like me. Especially my mentors, J. Elle and Tami Charles. I admire you both more than you know.

This book wouldn't have been written if it weren't for my amazing husband, Jay. You gave me the space, support, and time to write. I love you. Thanks to my dad, uncle Gary, and brother Steve for always being on standby anytime I needed some extra hands on deck.

I wouldn't even be a member of the Invincible Girls Club if it weren't for my wonderfully fabulous agent Natalie Lakosil, who thought I would be a great fit for this amazing project. And you were absolutely right. This project is a dream come true. To the incredible team who worked on this book—Alyson Heller, Anna Parsons, Addy Rivera Sonda, Heather Palisi, Ginny Kemmerer, Sara Berko, Amelia Jenkins, and Julie Doebler— thanks for bringing my words to life.

And last but certainly not least, thank you, Rachele Alpine, the fearless leader of the Invincible Girls Club. Not only did you welcome me with open arms but you gave me the green light to sprinkle my brand of magic into this incredible series.

I am honored to be included in this legacy.

—Steph B. Jones

Don't miss the next book!

THE INVINCIBLE GIRLS•CLUB

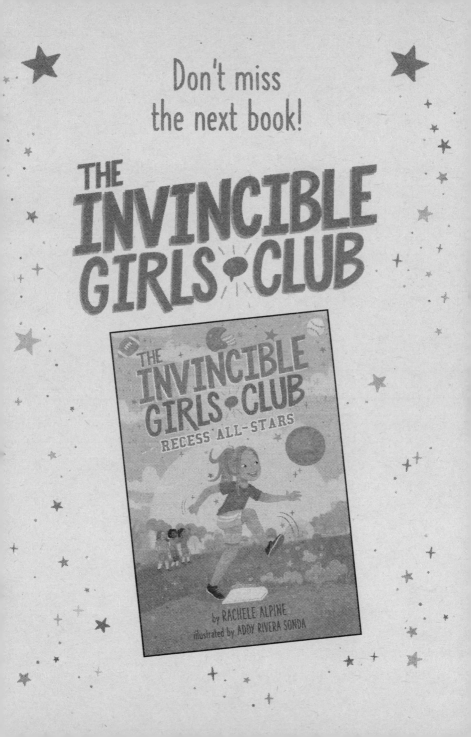

THE INVINCIBLE GIRLS•CLUB

RECESS ALL-STARS

by RACHELE ALPINE

illustrated by ADDY RIVERA SONDA

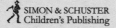

READ & LEARN

with *simon* kids

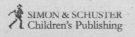